Serendipity

Dr. Vivek Kale

Published by Dr. Vivek Kale, 2024.

SERENDIPITY

First edition. April 24, 2024.

ISBN: 979-8224884490

Written by Dr. Vivek Kale.

Table of Contents

"To my dearest,

You are the inspiration behind every word, the muse that fills my heart with love and passion. Thank you for being my guiding light, my unwavering support, and my greatest source of joy. This book is dedicated to you, with all my love and gratitude, for your endless encouragement and belief in me.

Forever yours

KINTSUGI

You may have heard a quote, "The most beautiful souls are often the most broken." How can something be beautiful after it's broken?

.

Did you ever hear about 'Kintsugi'?

.

Kintsugi is the Japanese art of repairing broken things by mending the areas of breakage with powdered gold, silver, or platinum.

.

Japanese believe that being broken is not a bad thing. According to them the broken things can be repaired and reused as it was used before getting damaged. It embraces the flaws and imperfections, and you can make it an even stronger and beautiful by doing so. The same can be applied to life. Those cracks remind us of the mistakes we have done in the past and that repaired cracks are the depiction of what we learn from it.

.

It's completely okay to be broken. You can heal and can mend those cracks by a lot of things. But, in the end, sometimes it won't work. Because there are some cracks and voids which can't be fulfilled by others rather than that specific person or thing. Sometimes we fail to embrace the flaws and imperfection.

Love

I was born in the 20th century. A massive amount of technologies were developed in this century. 90's kids had seen dramatic growth & change in those technologies.

.

Now, in the 21st century, there are very few things that can't be bought. The mobiles, the fastest transport services, easy n effective connectivity are some things which shrunken the world and brought it closer.

.

Everyone now days are becoming slaves of the screens. Their world is so shrunken that it can be fit into a 4-6 inch screen. (Hell, what am I talking about, I'm also one of them. Writing this on my fucking smartphone screen.) Every idiot around me is busy with their smartphones. Hell, why am I saying like that, I am on a date with a beautiful girl and not all but some credit goes to my expensive smartphone and of course the premium Tinder membership and a strong internet connection. As I look around, mini-me asks me a question, "would it be possible without this technology?"

.

We are all trapped in this technology and materialistic world. We earn money and spent it on the expensive technology & stuff that we barely use or we get addicted to them. Most of the things we bought to show off a perfect life to total strangers. The things which don't last forever as the same as the premium

Tinder membership. (The love that lasts forever on a phone screen; and those phone screens need to charge again at the end of the day.)

.

"Hey, what are you thinking?"
She asked sipping her wine.

.

Oh fuck, I'm talking to mini-me (my inner self) again. I'm such a mess.

.

"Oh sorry, nothing."

.

I lied, how easy it is to lie these days. (On the phone screen & real life too.)

.

"What do you think about love and attention?"

.

"I think attention is the most basic form of love."

.

"And, why do you think so?"

.

"Love needs attention, it needs to be conveyed & expressed."

.

"Let's, suppose a relationship is a living organism then the attention is the basic food, and water."

.

"Attention is the basic need for a healthy & breathing relationship."

.

"Attention is a shelter and the root of relationship."

She took a sip and smiled.

I love her smile. Her smile is the prettiest thing I have ever seen. The top row of teeth was showing, and there was a faint curve to the lip. Her smile is a ray of sunshine and I am a sunburn.

The time stopped as my eyes met her gaze. Indeed, eye contact is a powerful stimulator of affection. I was feeling a connection. If it were anyone else I would drop my gaze, but with her, I'm drawn in closer. We were so still & calm, totally lost in each other.

Suddenly, my phone rang.

After taking my call while returning towards our table I realized that this mini idiot box works in two ways.
"You know what I think is, this universe might work in pairs", my inner me uttered.

I sit on the table and heard the ring again. I thought it was from my phone but thank God it was not mine.

"Yeah, I agree with you on that. This fucking smartphone is smart enough to get me a date but the same idiot is pulling me back from getting in her."

"Hey, are you there?"

"Yes", I lied again same as I lied to my friend just a minute ago on the call.

.

She smiles, this time I tried to move my eyes from her smile but I failed as my gaze stopped at her cute dimple. That smile is like a bliss. The perfectly aligned teeth, cute dimple, there was no crease below the eyes, just a slight movement of cheeks and the right touch of shyness which melted my heart.

.

" What do you think about forever?"

.

"Huh?"

.

"The forever kind of love people talk about?"

.

I took the sip & smile.

.

"Let me tell you something."

.

She adjusted herself to make me feel she was keen to hear what I had to say.
The kind of attention I talked about earlier, it seems to be reflected in her movements.

.

She adjusted her self to make me feel she was keen to hear what I had to say.
The kind of attention I talked about earlier, it seems to be reflected in her movements.

.

"My grandfather and grandmother first met each other at their mutual friend's wedding. They have been in a long-distance relationship for two years. (Nowadays long-distance relationship is way different than that era.) They were married for 75 years."

.

"Once my parents had a function to attain at night so they dropped me at my grandfather's place for a night. I was playing the game on my phone (which I got only for being connected with my parents whole the time). My Grandfather was reading a book, Grandmother was in the kitchen cleaning up the plates."

.

Her phone rang.

.

"Just a second. Sorry."

.

I smiled. (The screen again.)

.

"Sorry, please continue."

.

"Well, I was oblivious to everything busy with my screen. My grandfather kept a book aside and switched on the radio. He told me once that it was one of the best gifts from my grandmother. The song played- "Jab koi baat bigad Jaye."

.

"He walked into the kitchen, slowly took grandmother's hands, and wiped them with a towel. (Both were drawn in the eyes of each other.) Then he holds her closer and swayed in that little kitchen."

.

"I kept my phone aside & saw them- 75 years of love, togetherness, sweet talks, lovely fights, purest relation. And still, they could find love in the simplest of things."

.

"Maybe moments like these people tend to call- forever."

She smiled and we took a sip of one of the most expensive wines in the restaurant.

BONSAI

I was reading the book. My little sweetheart was enjoying the dreams. Somebody rings the bell on the door. I kept my book aside and got up from the chair and walked to the door. There was a delivery boy with a small pot plant of around 10-18 inches. It was sent by my beloved father. The delivery boy hand over me that pot plant and a letter.

That plant was so fascinating. I call my wife, she was so happy seeing that small tree. I put it on the table and opened the letter. I wondered Papa has sent me a letter. He can call me instead.

The reason behind not calling or texting and sending the letter is explained in the first second paragraph.

Papa had asked me, "Did you remember when you were in the fifth standard, you had a chapter in the Marathi syllabus about 'Bonsai'? (I didn't remember) Anyway, search it on google. (As I expected, he was sure about it.)

After searching it on Google, I got to know what it is. Don't worry you don't need to Google it, I'll explain.

"Bonsai" is a Japanese art form of tree cultivation. The literal meaning of 'Bonsai' is 'tray planting' (Bon=pot, Sai=plant). As an ancient horticultural art form that may be emerged originally in China (Back in 12th Century India, Bonsai was known and practiced as Vaman Vriksha Kala, or the art of miniature trees. It was used by Ayurvedic practitioners.) during the Han dynasty, the Bonsai art form went on to be developed in Japan.

.

Further on, Papa had written, "Bonsai trees are petite and fascinating. To me, they reflect sagacity that is both intriguing and profound. I'm sending you one as a gift for making me, grandpa."

.

"Imagine that you both are the Gardner of the Bonsai tree. The tree goes through several changes and mannerisms in its life and at each stage thrives. The aesthetic skills decide the future of that tree."

.

"Interpret the child-rearing as a representation of rearing and tending a Bonsai tree. The first goal of Gardner is to focus on the survival and health of the tree and then the artistic allure of the tree.

.

By survival and health, what I meant is to give your best to our child so that there is an unimaginable depth of possibilities that our child can visualize for their future. A future that will not only see a sense of contentment in what they do but how they can help others to attain that sense of contentment."

.

"Every parent tries to imbibe values in their children; from what they know and have learned in life. We did the same."

.

"But, we wish to imbibe the same values as ours but we never want you to be an identical version of ourselves."

"I think Bonsai trees are the symbol of retention of unique character. A character that emerges despite undergoing the guiding process of its gardener."

CORONA

It's been seven days since I tested positive for corona. Here I'm having a good time (Not that good). Hope you are having a good one.

.

I made a friend here (you read it read, I did). She is a sixty-year-old lady. She's so pretty and caring. They moved her to the intensive care unit yesterday. I miss her asking me about my morning over a cup of tea. Her smile makes my day brighter but I heard that she was in a lot of pain. But, I can't figure it whether it is physical pain or emotional pain that hurts her more. She talked about not seeing her son & grandson for the last three years. Her husband sacrificed his life for the nation during the war. Living alone in this old age with multiple diseases in pain and over it, this corona must multiply it umpteenth times. I wish her son and grandson should meet her before it's too late.

.

I think all she needs is a visit to love. Love that will erase all her pain. I don't know how I feel sad or bad but I'm missing her. I heard today that she had died of sepsis. How could someone leave her alone? She was so caring and loving to everyone here. How could her own son leave her all alone? Maybe she died three years ago when her son walked away. After that maybe she was just breathing...!!!

LIMITLESS

"What beautiful scenery!", she said looking out of the window.

I looked at her and smile. It was beautiful scenery indeed. We were on a road trip. I stopped a car at one of my favorite spots.

"Nature! Do we sit around nature anymore? Do you remember the last time when you met nature? Feel it?" She questioned me with a beautiful smile on her face.

"Well, I used to be", I said while going through my emails on my smartphone.

"Ohh, sitting around nature and busy on your phone, tablet, or laptop?" She said with that 'you dumb' type of gaze.

"Huh, sorry I had to send a very important mail."

"It's okay, just be with me when you are with me." She said.

That line reminds me of my ex.

We used to meet here at this beautiful spot. She loves the tulips more and I used to give her roses. She always complained about that and I always forget to get the tulips instead of roses.

She used to come here whenever she feels low. She comes here and calls me to be with her. But, sometimes due to some work I couldn't make it. Later when we met here again and I tried to ask her about it, she pointed to the stream and said, "the water never flows backward. It knows there's nothing left for it in the past".

.

She said that she loved to spend time here all alone but from the day we met she want me to be with her here.

.

Is there any limit to love someone? And what if you run out of it? Imagine if you love someone a lot but they left you (Left this world). And what if you spent a lot on someone and now you run out of it when some other person spending a lot of her love on you? No matter how wise or patient you are, you'll run out of it when you never get back the love you put in the world. And that lackness of love empty your heart and engulf your soul into the sadness and the pain.

.

She isn't here with me but I hope she is receiving a load of love up there.

.

She holds my hands and I suddenly brought myself back from those memories.

.

Maybe I'm not running out of it (love)...!!!

Derealization

It was just a six in the morning and I wake up. A way earlier than usual. I wake up and all I feel is a pain. It isn't physical. It's that kind of pain you feel after a night full of guilt and regret.

.

The house was empty and I can hear the tickling of my wristwatch. It was a gift from her. She is so punctual kind of person and I'm totally opposite. The 'tick-tock' of that watch and the 'thump-thump' of my heart making noise in my head.

.

I drag myself to the sink. Took my toothbrush and squeeze toothpaste on it, looking in the mirror. The eyes were wet, lower eyelids lifting the weight of the tears. Feeling tired. They say a hot shower is a tired body's best friend. It isn't today.

.

Every drop of shower reminds me of the words that I said to you. The words that hurt you. The pain that I'm experiencing is multiplying with every drop of water hitting on my body. It's cracking my body.

.

I make two mugs of coffee, forgetting that we are not together anymore. Maybe I thought that one extra mug will ain't make me feel lonely. I sat on a bean bag and kept one cup on the sofa; on the exact same place she used to put it. The coffee was getting colder with the memories we shared over the two mugs of coffee.

.

I checked my phone. Neither messages nor calls yet. I waiting for her message. Checking the screen over every couple of minutes. But there's nothing happening. Maybe sometimes we act to something or someone more than it has to be and in turn, we didn't get any reaction at all.

.

I kept my phone aside, walked into the kitchen. My stomach was empty. I couldn't make myself eat. I came near the refrigerator, looking for a note she left, but it wasn't there today. My stomach churns like my grandparents' old table fan. I take a bottle of beer and get my laptop for writing.

.

I sit for an hour and all I write (typed) is her name. Someone said it right, "A writer is someone for whom writing is more difficult than it is for other people." It's hard to express the helplessness I felt. My heart was thumping out loud. Maybe I was on a block; writer's block.

.

I put on the jeans and her favorite white shirt and blue jacket. It smells like her. I locked the room and get on the street. I wander for ten minutes on the streets undecided where to go. After some time I take a rickshaw to the railway station.

.

The guy on the ticket counter asked where I want to go? What would I answer him? My inner me screaming out loud- "to her". But I buried that scream deep inside and said "to the terminus!"

.

I sat on a bench for some time waiting for the train. The platform was so empty. After some time train arrived. I get on the train. The train was almost empty with few people here and there. I sit in the corner. I look around, trying to find someone with a similar kind of pain. Maybe they can help. But, I couldn't find anyone. A first station comes, I wish I see her get on. But she doesn't.

.

I was sitting in the same place for so long. The train goes from one end of the city to another, over and over. I lose count of the times the train crosses the same stations. My tired eyes were searching for her familiar face in every stranger that came in. But I didn't find her there. With the energy whichever left in me, I get down at my station.

.

It was almost night when I hit back home. The moonlight, trying to make the ending seem beautiful. I don't think all endings are beautiful. I tiredly made it to my home and abstractedly ring the bell and wait. I forgot she was not with me anymore and memories don't open doors. I used my keys and get in. I was so tired so I get in the shower.

.

I didn't make dinner though my stomach was empty. I slide in the bed on one side because I thought she will come anytime. I was lying on the bed like I was dead. I listen to the 'thump-thump' of my heart.

.

It was six in the morning when I woke up. I find us clasping each other in a warm, slow, and luxurious hug, I felt all oppositions to love had melted. My chest was rising and falling against her back, our breaths were in unison, and the warm blood that we could feel in each others' embrace.

ROLLERCOASTER

I am lying down in bed, awake at 3:30 am. Insomnia hits me hard but not harder than the memories. Sometimes I think it's not insomnia but the memories that kept me awake. I thought I could have written you a letter like Augustus wrote to the Hazel. Even though he is gone, that letter keeps reminding her of the love that has touched her life. And no matter how many times I read it, it always makes me closer to you.

Dear Augustus Waters and Hazel Grace Lancaster you were one of the five people we meet in heaven. Augustus, you wanted to be remembered by many and you feared oblivion. But, Hazel has a totally different perspective. And I am agreeing with her perspective. It is almost impossible to touch every person in the world even not half of them. I don't want to put a dent in the universe; I wanted to make a small space in your heart. Hazel teaches me that, it's okay to be loved deeply instead of widely.

Augustus, I love the way you enjoy metaphors. When you put that cigarette between your lips and you're this kind of behavior goes on Hazel's nerves. "You put the killing thing right between your teeth, but you don't give it the power to do its killing." This sentence of yours saying me like, I should have to use metaphors in life. Metaphors helped me to make sense of something that I haven't feel.

Hazel and Augustus both put my life on a different path at the time I got separated from you. Most I hardly remember and don't know how they changed my life. But you were the one I do.

.

I wish I had met you both and talk with you about the similar problems those we all faced and I am still facing. All endings are not happy. Everyone loves to believe in happy endings. That's how we were raised, isn't it? The fault in our stars shows that not all endings are happy and that not all wishes come true. Apparently, the world is not a wish-granting factory. Everything may not turn out as how I want it to be, I can enjoy the ride and make the most of it. I am on a roller coaster and I should aim for it to only go up.

PAIN

"You once asked me about pain, people, and forever. And I wasn't able to answer you at that time."

.

"I had both the people and pain by my side then. But, today standing all nil I think I can answer you."

.

"Oh stop, don't talk about people. I am so accustomed to people leaving me, that I almost assure you, that no one stays."

.

"You know we meet the people at every corner of the world.
Yeah, no one stays forever but there are some of many try harder to stay with us. We should…"

.

"Stop it; tell me about her."

.

"She, probably the greatest secret of my life as well as probably the most painful wound."

.

"Why your eyes are so glittering?"
I tried to change the topic but said something that my heart wanted to speak out for ages.

.

She resisted having eye contact and looked at the sky filled with stars.

.

"You know, we were amazing till it ended. Probably, a forever. But you know, this pain is/ was a lie, since it refused to stay forever. It oscillates only when I am drunk or when you aren't by my side. She is my scar now. It fails to make me burst into tears. But, yeah, sometimes open the flood gates of my memory leaving me to wonder why the things changed to do much."

.

She didn't respond. And when I saw her, she was just trying to control her tears. And that made my heart skip a beat.

I can't see her cry.

.

"Do love also leaves, when lovers decide not to stay together?"

I was stunned for a couple of minutes.

.

"Maybe, people get so much hurt by the love and when they try to get rid of that pain they stop thinking about the people they love and get rid of that love too."

.

She wiped her eyes and said with a cute smile, "look there, a shooting star, make a wish."

.

"You know, I always believed, I can never fall in love again but I did. And, today, I have got you. And I wish nothing more, only you."

MEANING

And here we are from where it all was started. The same café where I took you on our first date. I can't believe it is ending like this. I haven't imagined the journey that begins so softly will end so swiftly.

I still remember the day when I asked you for a date, I was so nervous thinking it's a bad idea. But, I think it wasn't one of the bad decisions I have ever made. I don't know why but I was happy that you were as nervous as I am. People who are too confident find it difficult to fall in love sometimes.

Damn, why did you have to wear that dress today? The same red dress that you wore on our first date which you've brought for Christmas. You smell better than the petrichor. Your habit of constantly trying to put your honey-kissed hairs behind ears while talking isn't changed.

You are the only girl who walks by me on the beaches and the only girl to sit on the back seat of my bike. Whenever you were on my bike, I wish that these roads should never end. But today, I'm walking you to the cab knowing very well that you won't walk with me anymore or won't be sitting on my bike anymore. I can't help but wish that these walk should last long.

I know I can't stop you. There have to be some words that could make you love me as much as I love you. Why I can't find it? Is it impossible to convey the feelings in the words?

As we reached the cab, I pull you closer and your face is as beautiful as it was on the first day we met. Maybe I won't able to forget your face though it'll be blurred in my tear-soaked eyes. And as I close the door of the cab those tears run down. My body goes numb, adrenaline rushes on and I gather all my feelings and push out of all a throat is "I Love You".

And for the first time, I realized how meaningless those words full of feelings can be.

TOGETHER

"Life is tough!",

.

"So, are you, sweetie."

.

.

.

Her doctor has scheduled a scan a week before usual.

.

She has to get an MRI every six months to check any new evidence of disease.

.

From the day I know I never saw her this much anxious and sad before.

.

"Hey, you don't have to worry everything will be fine."

.

"A lot of emotions and anxieties come up with this scan."

.

"Worrying is stupid, hope for good."

.

"Of course I hope that there aren't any new lesions."

.

A girl on the reception desk calls our name. And she went into the MRI room.

.

I stand outside that room praying for no more new lesions. What else can I do? Praying and hoping.

After forty-fifty minutes she came out of that room. She was nervous as I am.

.

"You know how it feels like when a build-up of the scan comes? I feel like walking on eggshells and every little step comes with a wave of worry."

.

"I'm in a constant battle with myself and mentally beating myself up before I know what the results are."

.

"You are the most positive person I ever met and it is exceptionally hard to get over this kind of worrying. But, hoping and praying is the best thing to do than worrying."

.

"I also don't want to worry but how do you stop worrying when your reality creeps up every six months?"

.

The tension in the waiting room was palpable as we both sat, enveloped in our thoughts, awaiting the results. Each passing minute felt like an eternity, laden with silent prayers and unspoken fears.

.

Finally, the doctor emerged with a serene yet inscrutable expression. "We've got the results," she said, her voice steady but giving away nothing.

.

Heart pounding, we both leaned in, our eyes fixed on the doctor, waiting for the verdict that could sway our world either way.

"I'm pleased to inform you that there are no new lesions," the doctor announced her words a balm to our anxious souls. "Everything looks stable and clear."

Relief flooded through us, washing away the weight of uncertainty we had been carrying for weeks. Tears welled up in her eyes as a smile stretched across her face, a radiant expression of gratitude and joy. I let out a breath I hadn't realized I'd been holding, a smile mirroring hers.

"Life is tough, but we're tougher together," she said, her voice brimming with relief and joy. Her eyes, usually vibrant with life, had been clouded with worry earlier, but now they sparkled with tears of happiness.

I couldn't help but echo her sentiment. "That's fantastic news," I said, reaching for her hand, feeling a surge of gratitude. The weight that had been pressing down on us seemed to dissipate with the doctor's words.

She had faced this trial with unwavering courage. Watching her battle her anxieties every six months during those scans, I felt a mix of admiration and helplessness. But today, her strength had triumphed.

As we stepped out of the clinic, the world felt renewed and more vibrant. The sun's rays seemed warmer, the sky a shade bluer. Holding her hand, I felt an overwhelming appreciation for every passing second.

"It's incredible how one moment can change everything," she said, gazing at the sky, her eyes filled with wonder.

"Yeah," I agreed, squeezing her hand gently, trying to convey the depth of my emotions. "Life is tough, but we've weathered it together."

The doctor's words echoed in my mind about living beyond the worry. It was a lesson, a reminder that amidst life's uncertainties, our love and hope were unshakeable pillars. We walked, hand in hand, down the street, the world bustling around us. But in that moment, it felt like time had slowed down, allowing us to savor the beauty of our togetherness.

MEMORIES

"It's a good thing I feel, being nervous."

.

"You know what, confident people find it difficult to fall in love."

.

Oh gosh! I write it wrong. We were into love, right? Maybe we are far beyond love.

.

I still remember those days when we used to go to our favorite café. Yeah, it was your favorite place, because you like that red velvet cake. I like to spend time in that café. Now, they stopped serving that cake. But, I still visit that place often.

.

I sit in a corner with memories. Those memories run in front of my eyes like a 3D movie. I can feel your presence there.

.

That very first meeting of our in that café, that ivory dress you wore the way you tucked your hair behind your ear. You seemed to be nervous, so am I.

.

Did you forget all the time that we spent together in that café? I still remember every moment that we spent here. The memories we created.

.

I would love to celebrate our birthdays here as we used to do.

.

I would like to read all those poems which you have written for me. Don't you miss those days when we sit there in the corner and I write short stories of us? I do.

.

Weren't we in love? I know I was, still, I am.

.

How could you let go? Maybe you got confident.

.

Maybe you cut your hair short.

.

"I still come here, sit in our favorite spot, because unlike us, memories never change."

BREAKFAST

Just months back I was searching for a rental house. And, she helped me to get one. It's been three months now I'm living here. Everything in this house is placed as per her.

.

I still remember that day when she argued with me because I shifted the bed towards the window.

.

Suddenly that scene encountered in my mind as I woke up to the sunlight on a winter morning. Back then she said to me to move the bed to the other wall but I denied it. I look at her and recall how beautiful last night was.

.

Her beauty was emerging with the rising sun rays. Her face was so beautiful. She was still sleeping I adjusted the blanket slowly dragging myself.

.

She didn't have any degree in interior designing but I feel like she is a master at it. I thought every woman is good at interior design in their way. Women are good at beauty & attractive things.

.

Our rental house was one big hall. Aarushi divided it into a bedroom & kitchen by a huge bookshelf. In front of the bed on the wall is a flat-screen which is hardly used whenever she comes over on weekends. There's a teapoy in the middle and two bin bags surrounding it for no reason. I barely sit on those bags. It was all her idea to buy those bin bags instead of sofas. And she was right at it that I hardly use the sofa to sit on. She is so attentive when it comes to buying something and I'm so careless at it.

.

I made my way towards the bathroom & brush my teeth & washed my face. Then I made my way to the kitchen. Filled the vessel & put it to boil. I took a bowl for mixing some eggs.

.

"Sweetie, how dare you to leave me alone in bed?" She asked leaning on the shelf looking at me.

.

I find her sleepy face more attractive than the normal one. My white shirt was perfectly hung on her curvy body though it was so loose. That white shirt was somewhat transparent showing a glimpse of her red lingerie. She did not bother to button it all the way. Her collar bones are so comfy I love to rest my chin over there. Her lips are like pink petals on rainy days. She did not like to wear makeup but she loves to use eyeliners. And her eyes with a hint of eyeliners are the most seductive part I ever discovered.

.

She clapped waiting for an answer. I make a move and slid her a mug of coffee and smiled.

.

"I thought breakfast in bed will please you. But, it seems like I'm wrong."

.

I knew that she loves to have coffee in the morning in the first place.

.

"Only if you are not making grilled cheese and scrambled eggs sandwich then you are right."

I motioned towards the eggs I was mixing.

.

She winked and made her way towards me after a couple of minutes.

.

"Well, you are are right though but I would prefer cuddles over breakfast." She uttered while hugging me from behind.

I turned to her & lift her and make my way towards the bed.

.

I kissed her and we cuddle for some time. Then I motioned back to the kitchen. She made her way to one of the bookshelves picking the book she was reading last night. She lay on the bed facing the kitchen sneaking glances at me. And I was busy making breakfast sneaking glanced at her.

TERMS & CONDITIONS

"It's over! I can't stand it anymore."

"What happened?"

"I don't wanna be with you, it's over."

"But,..."

Before I complete my words she takes her bag and left.

It's been two years now since that incident. But, I'm still can't get out of it.

When somebody asks me "Are you okay?", I reply "yeah, everything is fine." But deep down my mind says, "I'm not but everything is going to be!" But the other devilish mind end up with, "Am I going to be?"

I read and heard so many times that "you can't choose the people you fall in love with."
But, I haven't read or heard anyone say that "You can't choose to fall out of love."

Love can come and leave on its terms...!!!

HOPE

I leaned closer, the warmth of our intertwined fingers a lifeline amidst the emotional storm brewing around us. The rain outside mirrored the cascade of emotions within. We stood there, suspended between past regrets and a tentative hope for the future.

"It's not just about us, is it?" Her voice trembled, the vulnerability palpable. "It's about the trust we lost, the wounds that run deeper than words."

I nodded, acknowledging the depth of the fractures in our connection. "Rebuilding isn't easy," I admitted, tracing invisible patterns on her hand. "But maybe it's about learning to redefine what we mean to each other."

A faint smile danced on her lips, a fragile acknowledgment of the possibility ahead.

"Can we rewrite our story?" she asked, her eyes searching mine for a glimmer of certainty.

"We can try," I replied softly, holding her gaze. "One page at a time."

As the rain gradually subsided, a newfound sense of purpose enveloped us. We didn't know if our efforts would heal all wounds, but together, we were willing to brave the uncertainties, to rewrite our narrative in the gentle glow of newfound hope.

RENEWAL

I sat by the window, watching the rain paint intricate patterns on the glass. It was moments like these when my thoughts swirled in a tempest, echoing the complexity of emotions that had become my constant companion.

.

She stood by the doorway, her figure outlined against the soft glow of the room. There was a palpable tension in the air, an unspoken dialogue that lingered between us.

.

"I love you," I whispered, my voice breaking the silence that enveloped us.

.

Her eyes met mine, carrying the weight of regrets and the shards of errors that had fractured our path. "I love you too," she replied, her voice laced with a poignant sincerity.

.

The words hung in the air, laden with unspoken truths and unaddressed wounds. I longed to bridge the chasm that had widened between us, to mend what was broken, but the echoes of missteps reverberated in the space between us.

.

"Can we move past this?" I asked, the words heavy with a plea for reconciliation.

.

She hesitated, the turmoil within her visible in the furrow of her brow and the tremble in her voice. "I want to, but it's not easy. I've hurt you, and the scars of my actions are a barrier I don't know how to overcome."

.

My heart ached at her admission, understanding the depth of her remorse. "I know it won't be easy," I said, reaching out to take her hand. "But I'm willing to try. Together."

.

There was a flicker of hope in her eyes, a glimmer of belief that perhaps redemption was within reach. She intertwined her fingers with mine, a tentative gesture that spoke volumes.

.

"We both need to put in the effort," I continued, my gaze fixed on hers. "It won't be simple, but our love is worth fighting for."

.

As the rain continued its dance outside, we stood there, hands entwined, the unspoken promise of perseverance and mutual effort hanging in the air. In that moment, amidst the tumultuous emotions, there was a flicker of hope—a beacon guiding us through the storm towards a shared horizon of healing and renewal.

HARUKI

"I want to eat your pancreas." That way, I can be with you forever."

.

When you said it I felt what could be the most affectionate words than this to tell someone that you want to be with them?

.

It reflects the desire to cherish and hold onto the essence of the person you care deeply about, even after they're gone. It's a profound and intense way of expressing the longing for eternal connection and the fear of losing someone important. Believe me, I would have just simply said "I want to keep a part of you with me forever."

.

Sakura Yamauchi your perspective on life and death is astonishing. You know that you are facing mortality head-on and approach life with a mix of bravery, curiosity, and a desire to experience as much as you can in the time left. I got your word, "Every day is worth the same as any other. What I did or didn't do today doesn't change its worth."

.

And the way you define existence, no one could ever deny that. "If you're all alone, you can't tell that you exist. Your relationship with others is what defines being alive."

.

You portray both strength and vulnerability. You are not afraid to show your emotions, fears, or desires, yet you maintain a certain resilience that's inspiring. Meeting you could mean experiencing firsthand the impact you have on those around you. You form a unique bond with Haruki Shiga, changing his perspective on life, relationships, and mortality. Your relationships and interactions provide insights into the importance of human connections, how they shape us, and how they can endure even beyond physical presence.

I wish I had met you Sakura, interacting with you for discussions and explorations of themes such as life, death, friendship, and personal growth would have had an epic impact on me. You embody these themes in profound ways. Meeting you would offer a chance to delve into deep conversations, gain perspectives on life and mortality, and experience the emotional richness that comes from your unique character. But it won't be possible because you are just an anime character but you made an impact that changed me.

TACIT

Is it a feeling of being broken or the feeling of loneliness or emptiness that hurts the most? I asked myself this question several times.

.

After our rupture , I feel like I have loose something from my body, my heart still beats but I can't hear that lub dub sound anymore even in the complete silence.

.

I thought we share an unbreakable bond but maybe I was wrong about it. I asked you several times why but you didn't respond. You said silence is a very understandable language but I'm finding it difficult to get it. But, all I have learned after all of these consequences is that 'Silence is never the answer.'

.

Silence can be peaceful up to a certain extent but if it crosses the limits then it turned to the most annoying thing you ever come across. Silence for a long time can bring pain. Silence, secrets, and pain together form the most dangerous trio.

.

I can't figure it yet that was you the greatest secret of my life or betters the most painful wound.

UNSATISFIED

It's been half a month and I couldn't sleep well. It's not like I'm not tired enough to fall asleep. By the way who needs the tiredness to fall asleep all you need is peace.

.

While standing at the window taking in the last puff of my cigarette I decided to tell my father that my depression is back. I am aware that the conversation will not be smooth as always but I hope it should be a productive one and a conclusive one at the end.

.

I had to buy some novels. Nothing urgent. I could have bought them online but as one of my two friends told me I should stop wallowing in my misery and start going out a bit. So I convinced my father to take me to a book fair; after almost ten excuses which I've fought off. He had agreed and we were on the way. We were in Auto because he hates the parking. Here's how the conversation went if you care to know.

.

"So, you know how I said I need to go back on my medications a few months ago?" I started a bit vaguely.

.

"What? Medication? Your headache isn't fine yet?" He said, looking annoyed.

.

"No, it's not about a headache. I meant for my depression and anxiety." I muttered.

.

"But the Doctor already told you that you don't need to be on medication if you go early to bed and wake up early before sunrise. You'll be better then." He smiled.

.

"I go to the bed early but I can't sleep enough. And the problem is I can't get out of the bed itself." I cracked.

.

"But you wake up early today."

.

"That's because I hadn't showered in these days." The tears rolled down on my chicks. This was a mistake.

.

"You were going to visit Kritansh in Mumbai, no?"

.

The abrupt change in topic surprises me. "Yeah, but he has some work so the trip isn't final yet."

.

So, first, go on the trip. Have fun. After that, we'll talk about going to another Psychiatrist.'
He said.

.

While wiping my tears I asked, "What's the connection between my trip and the therapy."

.

Well, maybe after the trip you'll feel better and won't need medication."

.

"That's... That's not how it works." I sighed and whispered.

.

"This sweatshirt looks so great on you and you look stunning in it." He exclaimed putting his hand over my shoulder.

.

"Yeah, it was a good decision to buy them." I breathed.
"We're gonna reach, aren't we? I better grab my cash."

.

"Yeah, I looked out of the auto and calculating the days till I get financially independent to afford my psychiatrist appointment on my own.

.

Sometimes there's no satisfying end to a story. Just like life.

THEORY

"Stop it."

.

She screams snatching and throwing the book away. I look at her, my eyes blinking like a light bulb waiting to give up.

.

"Why do you love me so much?" she asks.

.

Before I could answer she throws off the blanket and gets out of bed. She makes her way to the window and stands there looking at the world, rather than staring into it. Maybe she felt that if she stared hard enough the world would blink and she'd win.

.

"Do you want me to make a list?"

.

I joke as I make my way near her, careful that I don't trigger her even more. We lean on two ends of a window and look at each other like two tracks of a train.

.

"You can do so much better than me."

.

She breaks the silence as she plugs a cigarette in between those lips. She doesn't light it but I know she wants to.

.

"Love is not finding who is perfect for us but rather finding someone who we can be imperfect with."

.

She taps her foot rapidly and then a hint of a smile crosses her face.

.

"Really? You can do better than a movie quote."

.

I move towards her and put my hand forward. She puts the cigarette aside and looks at me. I blink and her eyes water. I pick up the book, lift her, and make our way to the bed.

.

I read to her, 'Einstein says that everything has a dual nature so they can behave as a particle on some occasions and as a wave on some.'

.

I couldn't help but wonder if that's true with humans too. We tend to love and hate ourselves. On some days she only knows to do the latter. And on those days, all I could do is love her a little more.

.

I look at her, smiling through her tears, and continue reading to her.

.

INTOXICATION

It's something you'll never figure out as a friend or a nemesis.

.

You see it took a long time to learn to smile no matter how afraid or lost you are.

.

But once this thing passes through your lungs its compounds are absorbed into the bloodstream.

.

There, then it gets a grasp on your heart and ultimately the brain.

.

The heart you keep locked from this cruel world.

.

The brain that used to think its intelligence is its biggest enemy.

.

In a moment, the brain releases the dopamine, and you feel happy.

.

But that pleasure doesn't last long.

.

It makes to spill all your secrets. Secrets, that even though people claim they want to hear, will not understand.

.

And in the end, all these secrets do is drive them away, just like everyone else.

.

And you have to sober up, dust your heart, lock it, shake your brain, and find your smile again.

47

WISH

I used to think that talking over a cup of coffee is always a good idea until that day.

.

Her voice drowning my sobs. The two cups of coffee watching us like kids from broken homes.

.

"I don't want this anymore."

.

"But why? Would you at least tell me what's wrong?"

.

"Everything."

.

"What?"

.

We had been together for almost five years. I had recently left my job so I could focus on my writings. I'm doing a part-time job here at Naturals to pay my bills.

.

"We have different expectations from life. It's going to come in our ways sooner or later. And I can't wait till I find a way."

.

I don't blame her; everyone has a right to make a choice.

.

"We love each other. We will figure it out."

.

"Is it (love) enough?"

.

While grabbing her coat she hit the table and one of the coffee cups crashed down. I stand there looking at a single cup of coffee and several pieces of the broken cup.

.

The one who defines the love for me left me.

.

It was 6:20 pm already. I was late.

I found one of my co-workers at Naturals trying to calm down an elderly gentleman.

.

"I hate to say this but we run out of tender coconut flavor. Maybe you can try something else."

.

"No, If I want any other then why would I insist on this one?"

.

My coworker went to the telephone and enquired about that flavor at our other branches.

.

"Sorry, sir, we are out of stock. You can try another parlor."

.

"I don't want any other than Naturals tender coconut ice cream and I'm running out of time. Don't you get it?"

.

That old man yelled at him. He seemed disappointed. He looked around and feeling embarrassed and apologized.

.

" I'm sorry I didn't mean to. My wife is sick and she wants to have some Naturals tender coconut ice cream. I might lose her soon and I want to get her it soon in case it's her last wish."

While my coworker was telling him he doesn't need to apologize to him, a small girl came to him and whilst handing over the tender coconut ice cream said, "Grandpa, you can have this."

I tear up myself a little.

The old man broke into tears, hugged her, and kissed her on the cheeks.

"Oh, little angel thank you."

I saw the love in the purest form.

You defined a love right, "Love isn't something that breaks you, it's the something that puts you together."

DESPAIR

"Hey, I arranged a blind date for you."

.

"Listen, I don't need it and I didn't even ask you for it."

.

"Oh come on, hop on your bike and get your lame ass there. And be right on the time."

.

"Why don't you understand?"

.

"Don't be a brat, she must be enjoying her weekend already."

.

"So what, I still.."

.

"Don't be an idiot, you can't live in the past forever, just move on."

.

"Yes I can't; I can't live in there but I have been trapped in those moments. Every time I try to be with someone I try to find her in that person. And in the end, all I can find is despair."

DISTANCE

In distance's hush, your memory I keep,
    Without you, loneliness runs deep, so steep.

.

    Your smile, your laugh, like rain's gentle fall,
    Every moment with you, I crave it all.

.

    Your words' magic, sweet talks we'd share,
    In memories of you, my heart's laid bare.

.

    Long drives, days aglow with your grace,
    Your absence now, my heart's lonely space.

.

    Your solitude now, it tortures my mind,
    Desiring you, days and nights I find.

.

    Your cooking's sweetness, your cute tantrums too,
    I miss it all, longing for me and you.

.

    Yearning to meet, this heartache prevails,
    Distance strengthens love, as it unveils.

.

    I recalls, showers love in desire's blaze,
    Without you, my heart's in a daze.

SILENCE

Silence is annoying & peace-giving as well."
.

You can define noise as unpleasant, loud, disruptive or unwanted to hearing. But how will you define noise made by the silence?
.

Well, I know it's quite hard to understand. But, believe me, I've never been heard a noise harsher than the silence. Noise & silence are like the horizon. Like you can see the horizon but can't reach it.
.

The same thing has happened to me. I failed to differentiate between the silence & the noise when I was in the relationship. There was a time when I used to hear a noise in her silence & can feel the silence in her noise. But things changed after I've shifted to Hyderabad for my dream work. The long-distance took me away from that horizon. Earlier we used to talk for hours but later due to workloads and other reasons, I didn't get the time to contact her. The silence was getting heavy on our relation. That silence started to make the riotous noise between us. It was like a nightmare wrapped in the dream.
.

You were the one who told me the difference between 'silence' and 'quietness.'
.

You said that "the silence doesn't exist, but you can feel it solely when you can hear your heartbeat in the quietest environment surrounded by crowded emotions amidst the deep feelings."

And do you know what's the strangest thing is? After our breakup, I feel the silence but I'm unable to hear my heartbeats.

Don't miss out!

Visit the website below and you can sign up to receive emails whenever Dr. Vivek Kale publishes a new book. There's no charge and no obligation.

https://books2read.com/r/B-A-UBFIB-UVADD

BOOKS 2 READ

Connecting independent readers to independent writers.

Also by Dr. Vivek Kale

Serendipity

About the Author

Dr. Vivek Kale is a passionate writer and dedicated dentist who believes in the power of storytelling to inspire, connect, and transform lives. With a heart full of love and a mind teeming with creativity, Dr. Vivek explores the intricacies of human emotions, relationships, and the beauty of life through their writing.

Balancing the art of dentistry with the craft of writing, Dr. Vivek brings a unique perspective to their work, drawing inspiration from the diverse experiences encountered in both fields. Whether crafting compelling narratives or tending to patients' oral health, Dr. Vivek is committed to making a positive impact on the lives of others.

Driven by a deep desire to share their experiences and insights with the world, he invites readers on a journey of discovery, reflection, and growth. When not lost in the world of imagination or tending to patients, he can be found indulging in their other passions, which include reading, transforming smiles and cooking.

Above all, he is grateful for the opportunity to connect with readers, patients, and communities alike, and share in the magic of storytelling and oral health together."

www.ingramcontent.com/pod-product-compliance
Lightning Source LLC
Chambersburg PA
CBHW021319160726
47994CB00004B/1519